# Elephant in the Kitchen

by WINSOME SMITH

Illustrated by CAROL NICKLAUS

SCHOLASTIC BOOK SERVICES

NEW YORK • TORONTO • LONDON • AUCKLAND • SYDNEY • TOKYO

ISBN 0-590-32470-5

12 11 10 9 8 7 6 5 4 3 2 1          2          2 3 4 5 6 7/8
                    Printed in the U.S.A.                    11

# CONTENTS

## Angry Beginnings

"I want *my* name at the top of the poster!" screamed Le Vram the magician. With each word his face grew redder.

"But you are *not* the star of this circus!" Mr. Borrill, the circus owner, thumped the table with a fat fist.

Mr. Borrill and Le Vram stood nose to nose in Mr. Borrill's trailer. Every time Mr. Borrill thumped on the table, the trailer shook.

"This poster is an insult!" shouted the magician. He grabbed a poster from the table and waved it in Mr. Borrill's face. "I suppose you think that that elephant, Cato, is the star of the circus."

"Cato *is* the star," Mr. Borrill said. "You're not—not by any means. I asked Sam Fleming to make the poster this way."

Mr. Borrill snatched the poster from Le Vram. "Come to Borrill's Circus," he read in a loud voice, "starring Cato, the Amazing Elephant.

"In my circus I've got trapeze artists, acrobats, performing horses, dogs, and lions," he said. "I've got clowns, tumblers, and a man who eats fire. They're all great performers, but the main attraction is Cato, the elephant. He's the star. I would put *all* my performers on that poster before the name of a second-rate magician."

"Second-rate!" Le Vram's face turned from red to white.

"Of course," said Mr. Borrill. "Remember the time you got a boy from the audience to help you, and he was better at magic than you were? Remember the time you went to pull a rabbit out of a hat, and the rabbit wasn't there? Remember the time you tried to make a lady disappear, but you blew the lights, and the whole circus went dark? Your magic doesn't work! Magicians don't belong in circuses anyway. I only gave you the job because I felt sorry for you."

*Da-da-da-BOOM-da-da* came from the big top nearby. Then the music stopped. There was a sound like lots of leaves flapping in a strong wind.

"Hear that sound?" asked Mr. Borrill. "That's applause. That is the sound of many people clapping, and if you listen carefully you will also hear the laughter of children. They are enjoying my circus and, if I'm not mistaken, clapping for more of Cato. And that is why Cato is the star of my show. He gets applause. You don't."

"I'll ruin you for this." Le Vram was no longer shouting. "The Great Le Vram called second-rate? I'm leaving, but you'll pay for this outrage. I'll show you whether or not my magic works."

Le Vram rushed out of the trailer. He banged the door so hard that Mr. Borrill's bright new posters scattered across the floor.

The angry magician stamped down the wooden steps and hurried off toward his own trailer.

"Thunderation! Thunderation! Hurricane, pestilence, and devastation!" Le Vram flopped on the steps of his trailer, muttering to himself.

"Rabbits out of hats . . . disappearing ladies. . . . That foolishness is not for me, the Great Le Vram. No—evil is my specialty— evil and revenge. Evil spells that really work. They *work*, I say! That is, unless there is too much . . . too much . . . goodness around. Yes, too much goodness, kindness, thoughtfulness, and generosity. Too much of that is the only thing that can spoil my magic."

He stopped. More laughter and cheering came from inside the big top.

"Little children laughing! Thunder and plague! Imagine me, with all my ancient and dreadful skills, working in a circus. Making little children laugh. Bah!"

Suddenly he slumped on the trailer steps. "It's too much for me. I'll retire, that's what I'll do. I'll retire to my house in the mountains. But first of all—REVENGE! I'll ruin Borrill and his circus. People who upset magicians deserve to be ruined. I'll show them. They can't treat *me* like this."

## The Last Act

Inside the big top the audience was enjoying the show. In one of the front seats John Darcy straightened his glasses so he could see the last part of the elephant act clearly.

His uncle, Sam Fleming, had painted the posters for the circus. So John Darcy had a free seat and had gone to every show since the circus came to town.

Now John looked around and decided that the elephant act was everyone's favorite. The children laughed and applauded as Cato stole a cap from a little boy's head and waltzed around the ring waving the cap in the air. A clown, pretending to chase one of the elephants, tripped on a rope and rolled over in somersaults.

John Darcy had overheard Cato's trainer

say that Cato was too lazy to do his tricks properly in the ring, even though he knew how to do them very well. This seemed to be true, because whenever the children laughed at a mistake, Cato made another, and another, until the whole audience was in an uproar. But if nobody laughed at a mistake, Cato went through his act perfectly, never taking a wrong step and obeying every command. John thought Cato must be a very clever elephant. He knew exactly when to make mistakes and when not to.

In the bandstand, the musicians blew into brass instruments, twiddled with keys, and tapped with drumsticks as Cato's act drew to a close.

"Encore!" shouted someone in a back seat.

*Da-da-da-BOOM-da-da,* played the band. It was the signal for Cato to return and do some extra tricks.

The audience cheered as he lifted a surprised circus worker off his feet and then stole a bag of peanuts from the peanut vendor.

At last Cato was led to the main exit. The trapeze act finished the show. When the circus

was over, Cato would nod good-bye to the people as they walked out.

Across the ring from John, a tall, thin man with a bushy black beard sat on a high wooden stool. He was John's uncle, Sam Fleming. He had a sketch pad on his lap. Every time he finished a page, he would tear it off the pad and start a fresh one. He worked quickly. There was so much in the ring that he wanted to draw.

Stella Borrill, the circus owner's daughter, stood next to Sam. She had been around the circus ever since she was a little girl. She had worked on the tightrope for a while, but now she helped to run the circus and look after the money side of things.

"You've drawn the elephants beautifully," she said to Sam, "especially Cato."

"I wanted to show how graceful and clever they are," Sam said.

"That's just what you've done." Stella picked up some loose pages from the ground and looked at them again. Although these were only quick sketches, she could see the kind of paintings they were going to be. Sam's trapeze artists seemed about to swing right off the page. His horses leaped and pranced so that their hooves seemed to twinkle. The sketch of the balancing act showed every straining muscle.

"This is the circus, Sam," she said. "You've caught it on paper."

Sam grinned.

The band changed from dance music to a marching tune. The circus was over. The audience began to move slowly toward the exits.

John Darcy left his seat and, stepping over the ropes, made his way across the ring to Sam.

Over at the main exit, Cato nodded his head and swayed his trunk as the people filed past him. His bright little eyes sparkled as the children patted him. They gave him peanuts or potato chips or cookies. He took them in his trunk and put them into his mouth.

Near the main ring, John said hello to Stella, then turned to Sam. He straightened his glasses to look at Sam's last drawing.

"Hmm, not bad, Sam," he said. "Oh, Mom told me to remind you about tonight."

"What about tonight?" Sam added a few lines to his sketch.

"You're coming to our house for dinner," John told him. "Mom said that if I don't remind you, you'll forget."

Sam laughed. "I can never convince my sister that I really do eat very well. She thinks I can't look after myself."

The tent was almost empty. The circus workers hurried to clean up for the evening show. Sam put his sketches into a flat card-

board folder and tied it with tape. Then he began packing his equipment in a battered old suitcase, while Stella and John waited.

Suddenly, Le Vram pushed past them, knocking Sam's case to the ground and scattering his pencils and pads in the sawdust. He rushed across the ring and charged out the main exit.

"Hey, watch what you're doing!" Sam yelled.

As Sam and his friends shook the sawdust out of the sketch pads and gathered up the pencils, they heard a startled cry from the exit. The elephant trainer was waving his arms wildly.

"Call Mr. Borrill!" the trainer shouted. "Get the police! Do something . . . anything! Cato has disappeared!"

# Where's Cato?

Mr. Borrill was still angry about his argument with Le Vram when he heard a frantic knocking at the door of his trailer. He opened the door to find a clown, gasping for breath.

"What do you want?" Mr. Borrill snapped.

"Cato has disappeared!" the clown said. "You'd better come to the big top right away."

"Ridiculous! It's impossible to lose an elephant. Go back and find him." Mr. Borrill banged the door shut, then immediately opened it again.

"I'm sorry," he said, "I'm not usually like this. It's just that I've had an upsetting afternoon. Come on, we'll look into this together."

They hurried across the grass to the big top.

"It looks like a case for the police," the clown said.

"Elephants don't disappear." Mr. Borrill lifted the curtain and entered the big top. "Let's not lose our heads."

Circus people wandered to and fro around the big top, calling, "Cato, Cato."

"This is silly," John Darcy said. "There is absolutely nowhere for an elephant to hide in here. He must be outside among the trailers and cages."

Clowns, acrobats, and jugglers, still in their costumes, followed John out of the big top. They rushed about, bumping into each other, and calling Cato's name.

Someone had called the police, and two young officers showed up. They had dealt with robberies and lost children, but neither of them had ever been asked to search for a lost elephant. They weren't at all sure how to go about it.

The officers asked everyone a lot of questions and wrote things down in their notebooks, but they didn't come up with a single clue.

Mr. Borrill took out his handkerchief. "This is the worst thing that has ever happened to me," he said to Stella. "If Cato isn't found our circus will be ruined."

"Don't look on the gloomy side, Father," said Stella. "You said yourself that elephants don't get lost. Let's get ready for the evening show. The circus can go on, even without Cato."

"Nonsense, my dear. The time has come for us to face facts. All that laughing and cheering, all those happy faces are only because of one performer . . . Cato. He is a real actor, that elephant. He even makes his mistakes look funny."

Mr. Borrill blew his nose. "The children love Cato. And it is children's joy that *makes* a circus."

# Elephant in Danger

Cato was just as puzzled as everyone else. He had been standing by the door of the big top, the way he always did, nodding and swaying as the crowd shuffled past.

The last of the children had patted him, and he had eaten the last peanut. He stood waiting patiently for his trainer. He was looking forward to a nice meal of hay and a good rest before the evening show. The workmen were busy tightening ropes and sweeping up.

When Le Vram rushed into the tent, Cato saw that the magician was in a temper. But there was nothing unusual about that. Cato simply went on thinking about hay and peanuts and the way the children had clapped for him.

Then Le Vram stopped in front of Cato. He reached up and put his hand on the elephant's trunk. The magician had never done this before, but Cato had been patted so often that afternoon that one more hand made no difference. Le Vram moved on and left the tent.

Unusual feelings swept over Cato. One minute he was standing in the circus tent, and the next minute he was surrounded by a forest of grass—so tall that it was over his head.

Feeling stranger by the second, he shook his legs one by one. First he shook his right front leg, then his left front leg, then he shook his right hind leg. It was when he shook his left hind leg that he realized something was definitely wrong. The chain he always wore around his ankle was missing.

I'm in the jungle, Cato thought. It's magic. I've been taken from the circus and moved to the jungle.

Tall grass waved about him. He began to push through the grassy forest, but soon his way was blocked by a pile of rocks. He stopped for a moment to think. Should he go to the left or to the right? Where did he want to get to anyway? How was he going to get back to the circus? If he kept walking, he might soon come to a river or a road or even a herd of elephants. That would be nice. It was rather lonely in this strange jungle.

Walking closer to the rocks, he saw they were red and green and gold—and almost transparent. The rocks sparkled with a fine coating of silvery dust. More dust was scattered on the ground and it glittered in the jungle grass.

Carefully, Cato stepped around the bright boulders. Behind them was the tall, narrow entrance to a cave.

Cato put out his trunk and waved it around inside the cave. There was a sweet smell—not unpleasant and strangely familiar.

Suddenly the sky darkened. A shadow fell across the earth. The ground shook. Thunder rolled. Cato crouched in the entrance of the cave waiting for the rain to start. Instead of rain, an enormous object crashed into the long grass.

A trailer? wondered Cato. It was as big as a trailer, but was a shabby brown, not brightly painted like the circus trailers. The tires at

the back were not round. They were long and
thick and straight, just like the heel of a . . .

Cato shuddered. He was looking at a giant
boot.

But why would such a gigantic boot be here
in the jungle? Cato stepped into the cave,
bumping against a red boulder. It rolled gently
to one side, and Cato saw that it was not
hard—it was soft.

Then he realized why that sweet smell was familiar. Those rocks were gumdrops coated with sugar. This cave was the gumdrop package dropped by some careless person. He was not in the jungle after all. He was still at the circus!

Cato looked around and saw that the boot was attached to an enormous leg. A short distance away was another leg, and both were attached to a man whose head was so far up that Cato could barely see it. The head turned, and Cato saw it was his trainer.

Something strange had indeed happened. Cato had not been moved to another place. He was still here in the circus—but he had shrunk! He was as tiny as a mouse.

The thunder still roared above him, but Cato now recognized it as voices—human voices.

"Call Mr. Borrill! Get the police! Do something . . . anything! Cato has disappeared!"

"Cato, where are you?"

"Cato, Cato."

The tiny elephant's heart was pounding. He had never felt so afraid. He knew he could be crushed at any moment by rushing feet. Where could he hide?

Peering up through the grass, he saw the doorway of the big top—a doorway through which, at any moment, people might run. Giant people. A cardboard box could not protect him.

There should be a curtain nearby. Cato turned around. Yes, there it was, right behind him. He lifted it with his trunk and struggled under. He knew he should now be under the seats.

He looked up again. Sure enough, the planks of the seats rose in steps above him. He would be safe here for a while, at least.

But not for long. He heard gusts of wind, as a panting dog sniffed at the ground near him. Wheels creaked as cages were rolled around. Feet thundered by. The circus had once meant home and safety and friends—but now it meant only danger.

Among the sounds, Cato heard Mr. Borrill's worried voice. "He can't be lost. We'll search everywhere. Look behind the trailers, behind the trucks, among the small cages. Look behind every curtain in this tent. Cato must be found!"

People began to move things around. That meant even more danger. At any moment a heavy box, crate, or plank could land right on top of him. Everyone was looking for a large elephant, not a tiny one.

Not far away, Cato saw an open suitcase. It was as big as a house, and it lay tipped against some ropes. There were enormous sheets of paper and huge pencils spilling out. Cato thought he'd be much safer there, away from those great, hurrying feet. When the noise and shouting had died down a little, he ran toward the suitcase. He walked up a bundle of ropes to the edge of the case. Carefully he stepped from the rope onto some sheets of paper and, with a gentle thud, slid down among pencils, erasers, sketch pads, and drawing charcoal.

He snuggled among the drawings and listened to the sounds around him. Voices shouted, boots thudded, dogs barked. In the distance lions roared. He reached out with his trunk and pulled a sheet of paper over himself.

He felt safe here. He stayed quite still under the paper while everyone from the circus looked for him.

Suddenly there was a sharp bang and everything was dark. The lid of the suitcase had been closed. The case was lifted into the air, and Cato was thrown upside down.

Sam Fleming, without knowing it, carried Cato away from the circus.

## Arriving Home

"I can't get over it," John Darcy said, as he and Sam walked home. "I thought it would be impossible to lose an elephant."

"Just look at that sunset," Sam murmured. "I could paint that in shades of gold and apricot." In one hand he carried his case, which swung as he strode along. His big folder of drawings was tucked under the other arm.

"I mean, they're so big they're easy to see," John Darcy said.

"Of course they are," Sam said. "They fill the whole western sky."

"Elephants in the sky?"

"No, sunsets," Sam said. He looked down at his young nephew in surprise.

"The trouble with you, Sam, is that you can't

think of anything except drawing and painting. I wasn't talking about sunsets. I was talking about losing things."

"Oh, of course," Sam said. "That's not unusual. I lose lots of things."

"Don't I know it! I help you search for things all the time. But you lose things like pencils, socks, cash, tubes of paint. You've never lost an elephant, have you?"

It was getting dark, and lights were coming on in the windows of the houses they passed.

Although the town was small, the walk home took a long time because Sam had so many friends. He stopped to chat with Nick at the fish market and the man at the fruit stand. He said hello to everyone he passed.

By the time they got home, the movie theater across the road was open, but people had not yet begun to line up at the ticket window.

John Darcy lived with his widowed mother in a neat, pretty cottage. Sam Fleming lived in a ramshackle studio he had built in their backyard.

Mrs. Darcy often tried to get her brother to

move into their spare room, but he always refused.

"There might be room for me in that spare room, Annie," he would say, "but where would I put my paints, my paintings, and drawings? Anyway, you like things tidy. You couldn't stand having someone as messy as me in your house."

Mrs. Darcy knew he was right, but she still worried. She was sure Sam could not look after himself. So she made him puddings and soup and brought him fruit. She darned his socks (when they could be found), and she sometimes insisted he come to dinner. Mostly, though, she left him to do his painting in the happy mess of his tumbledown home.

"My goodness, you two are late!" she said when Sam and John Darcy finally arrived. "I got back from the Children's Home Committee meeting ages ago. There's a casserole in the oven. I've got some important news for you, Sam."

"And we've got news for you, Mom," said John. "There's an elephant missing from the circus and —"

"Yes, dear. Tell me all about it while we eat. Sam, where are you going?"

"Some idiot knocked my case over at the circus, Annie. I'll just check that the sketches are still okay."

"Well, don't be too long," said his sister.

Sam rushed into his studio, dropped his folder on the floor, and flung his suitcase onto the kitchen table. He switched on the light, opened the suitcase, and picked up the top sheet of paper.

"This one's got dirt on it. I'll have to throw it out." He crumpled up the sheet and dropped it on the floor. "Now, let's see. Did that charcoal stick fall out?"

"Sam!" John Darcy called from the doorway. "Sam, Mom's waiting—and I'm starving. Come and eat."

"Well, all right. I can fix this up later," said Sam.

He left the suitcase open on the kitchen table and hurried out.

## Hay in the Kitchen?

Cato listened. Everything was quiet in the studio—except for the *plop, plop, plop* of a dripping tap. When he was sure no one was there, he pushed aside some papers and stood up. Cato felt stiff and bruised and cranky. He wanted to be back at the circus having a nice meal of hay and perhaps a few apples.

Cato climbed onto the piled-up sketches, then stepped down onto the suitcase's open lid. He walked down the lid, climbed over the edge, and found himself, if not on firm ground, at least on a firm kitchen table. He stretched his aching limbs and had a good look around.

So this is what the inside of a house looks like, he thought to himself.

Sam's home had only two rooms—a studio, where he worked and slept, and a kitchen, where he cooked. A doorway separated the two rooms.

Cato looked into the studio. He saw a big, untidy, muddled workroom. In the middle of the studio, there was a large table covered with paint tubes, jars of brushes, old paint-covered rags, sticks of charcoal, and unfinished sketches.

Sam's clothes, coffee mugs, and paintings were scattered from one end of the studio to the other. Even Sam's bed had a pile of pictures stacked on it.

From the kitchen table, Cato could just see a window along the side wall of the studio. It was almost as big as the wall and looked out on the movie theater across the road.

Sam's kitchen was another happy mess. In the middle there was the table that Cato was standing on. Beside this table was a sink, and on the other side of the sink stood an old-fashioned cupboard.

It was a battered old cupboard—so old that it leaned to one side. The counter was littered with household and art supplies of every possible kind.

Nearly every letter that Sam had ever received had been thrown unopened onto the counter. Sam hated opening letters, because they were usually bills. A leather wallet lay open, with money and papers falling out. There were saucepans, a package of cheese, a carton of eggs, and one brown suede shoe. A gray woolen sweater lay among some tubes of paint, with one of its sleeves hanging down over a deep cupboard drawer. The cupboard counter was worn. In one place the wood had split open, leaving a large hole.

Although Sam always washed his dishes, he hardly ever put them away. Cups, plates, mugs, and silverware littered the table where Cato stood. There were also boxes of crackers, bread on a breadboard, apples in a dish, a coffee mug full of paintbrushes, and pencils in a jam jar.

Again Cato heard the *plop, plop, plop* of water. The tap over the sink was dripping. Feeling very thirsty, he started toward the tap.

Sam's wire dish drainer stood in the sink. It made a handy ladder down into the stainless steel sink, so Cato climbed down.

Little puddles of water lay here and there

on the bottom of the sink. Cato took a long drink. Then he stood under the dripping tap and let the water run over him. It trickled over his head and neck and back and settled in little pools around his feet. It felt cool and clean and fresh—almost as good as being under the hose.

Then he remembered that Sam might soon come back. He climbed up the dish drainer and looked in the kitchen cupboard, hoping to find something to eat. He didn't expect to find any hay, but there just might be something tasty.

Behind the suede shoe he found a half-empty can of spaghetti. He dipped in his trunk, and

pulled out a short, soft, juicy rope. Not bad, he thought as he tasted it. Not bad at all.

Just as he was finishing the last of the spaghetti, he heard a noise. It was the sound of footsteps. Remembering those huge boots that nearly trampled him at the circus, his first thought was safety.

The footsteps came closer. Cato took a few short steps, slipped, and fell forward. Air rushed past his ears. He heard a gentle rustling sound as he rolled over onto his feet. He looked around. He had fallen straight through that hole in the counter top and was now inside the drawer, standing on a pile of tracing paper.

The studio door opened with a creak, then closed again. Cato hid in the paper and listened.

# Elephant in the Newspaper

"That's what the man from the town council told me, Sam," said Mrs. Darcy as she and John followed Sam into his kitchen. "He believes this place is unsafe and has to be pulled down before it falls on top of someone."

"Annie, did you explain to him that this is my home? I built it myself."

"Of course I did," she answered. "I thought the man was very rude telling me my backyard was an eyesore. It didn't make any difference though. He said that if you don't pull it down, the council will come and pull it down for you."

John Darcy leaned against the sink and looked around. The building was an eyesore. Sam was a good artist, but he was not a very good builder. The roof leaked, and there were cracks in the walls.

John Darcy noticed a row of wet dots going from the sink to the cupboard. He leaned a little closer. *I wonder how that happened,* he thought.

A soft rustling sound came from the cupboard drawer. *Mice,* he thought.

While his mother and Sam talked, John Darcy moved over to the cupboard. The same round wet dots were on the counter top. *They certainly aren't mouse tracks,* John said to himself, but nothing else would be small enough to be rustling around in a cupboard drawer.

He put his hand on the drawer handle and pulled. Nothing happened. The drawer was stuck. The cupboard leaned so far to one side that the drawer was jammed shut.

He pulled the handle again. He rattled it. The drawer stayed closed.

"Sam, do you know you've got mice?" he said.

"Mice!" Mrs. Darcy said. "I wouldn't be surprised if you had whole families of mice in those cupboards, Sam. Have you ever cleaned them out?"

"Of course I have. I cleaned them out only three years ago. I can guarantee there are no mice there."

"Just look at those gaps in the roof," Mrs. Darcy went on. "Sam, dear, I think the council is right. You'll have to move into the house and pull this place down, before there's an accident."

"That's impossible," said Sam. "It's a kind offer, but there isn't room for me and all my equipment in your house."

"Then you'll have to buy or rent another place," said his sister.

"You know I haven't got any money. Just about every cent I earn is spent on art supplies." Sam picked up his folder from the floor and began sorting his sketches.

"That's ridiculous! You just don't look after your money. You should have thousands saved up. Haven't you got a bank account?"

"I never have any money to put into the bank," Sam said. He held up one of his circus sketches. "Just look at this. Isn't she beautiful?"

It was Stella, poised on a tightrope—a pic-

38

ture of perfect balance. Below her was the dizzy mass of upturned faces in the crowd. The whole background was blurred, just as Stella, glancing down, might have seen it.

Mrs. Darcy admired her brother's work a great deal. She took the picture in her hands to get a closer look.

"Yes, it is very well done, Sam," she said. "I don't know how it is that you haven't got plenty of money when you do work as good as this."

The next morning John Darcy rushed into the studio waving a newspaper.

"Just look at this, Sam."

Sam was standing at an easel working.

"Something about Cato?" he asked.

"A lot about Cato," John answered.

Sam read aloud:

ELEPHANT LOST
Strange Disappearance
of Circus Favorite
Local police are baffled by the mysterious disappearance of an elephant from Borrill's Circus late yesterday afternoon. . . .

"So he hasn't been found yet," he said.

"No," John answered. "There's a lot more in the newspaper story—and look above the story. There's a photograph of Mr. Borrill and Stella."

"So there is. And under that it says: 'Mr. Borrill told reporters that without Cato his circus would be ruined.' "

"Well, I've got to get to school early to change my library books. Mom said to remind you that the man from the council is coming to see you today. And keep an eye out for that elephant."

Sam Fleming and John Darcy were not the only ones to show great interest in the headlines that morning.

In an old brick cottage surrounded by an overgrown garden, in a town in the mountains, Le Vram read the news about Cato over and over again.

"Strange Disappearance," he read aloud for the fifth time. A little twinkle came into his eyes. "I did it," he said. His mouth twitched into a grin. "I made something disappear." He leapt to his feet. "I did it!" he shouted. He laughed out loud and skipped about. "At last I've done the Ancient Disappearing Trick. I made something disappear."

He ran to a bookcase near the window and began to rummage among the old leather-covered volumes. He laughed and said again, "I performed the Ancient Disappearing Trick. I am great after all."

He chose one of the books and sat down at the table.

"Now if only I could remember what spell I used," he said, turning the pages. "I was in such a state I said the first thing that came into my head."

Le Vram searched through the book for a while. Finally he smiled and said, "I can't find the spell right now. But what does it matter? I did it. Making an elephant disappear is no small trick."

He picked up a pair of scissors and carefully cut out the article about Cato.

## Cato Follows His Trunk

Earlier that morning Cato woke up to find himself lying on sheets of paper instead of his usual bed of straw. Then he remembered he was not at the circus anymore. There had been a dizzying ride, swinging through the air, then a drink of water and a shower, followed by a meal of soft, thick ropes from a can.

Now he seemed to be in a big wooden box. There was a hole in the roof of this box. The sunlight shone in, faintly lighting up everything inside.

Cato stretched and lifted his trunk. He flapped his ears. Then he remembered that something had made him tiny.

Cato looked around. He saw stacks of pencils held together with rubber bands, sheets of white drawing paper, and erasers. Letters, some opened and some unopened, had fallen through the hole into the drawer, just like Cato.

If I'm going to stay here, I have to be comfortable, Cato thought. He was used to helping when the circus gear was being packed and unpacked, so he knew what to do. He collected all the pencils with his trunk and piled them at one end of the drawer. He stacked some of the tracing paper to make a soft bed near the front of the drawer.

Pieces of greenish-colored paper with pictures and numbers on them were scattered about the drawer. He stacked them all in a corner.

After a while he realized it was breakfast time. Last night, before he had fallen through the hole, he had seen plenty of food.

He looked up at the strip of light above him. I've got to get up there somehow, he thought.

When he was straightening the drawer, Cato had found a long piece of wood with little black lines and numbers along one side. Lifting this board with his trunk, he leaned it against the edge of the hole. He placed one foot on the board, but it wobbled.

He needed something to hold it firm. He reached out and pulled two erasers toward him. He jammed these against the end of the board. Then he tested the board again. This time it did not move.

Carefully, Cato took a step forward and upward. He took another step, and then another.

This is great, he thought. Now I can get out and find something to eat. I might even be able to find my way back to the circus.

At the top he slowly pushed his head through the hole. More pieces of colored paper with printing on them slipped past him and fell into the drawer.

There was a sudden loud noise. The back door opened, and in rushed an enormous boy wearing thick glasses. He was waving a newspaper.

"Just look at this, Sam!" the boy shouted.

Cato quickly pulled his head back through the hole. Now he could not see the people in the room, but he could still hear what they were saying. He heard his name. They were talking about him.

"So he hasn't been found yet," he heard Sam say.

Cato wanted to shout, "I'm here. Look over here!" Instead, he stayed on the board in his drawer. Who would believe that a tiny elephant found in a kitchen drawer was the famous Cato, the circus favorite?

Sadly he climbed backward down the board. He wondered if he would ever get back to the circus. He thought of the sweet smell of hay, the feel of sawdust under his feet, the excitement of being in the ring, the sounds of laughter and music. Would he ever enjoy them again?

As he reached the bottom of the board, he thought: Anyway, I'm glad I'm a circus elephant and not a jungle elephant. Only circus elephants know how to walk on boards and do the things I have learned to do.

He still had not had any breakfast, but he had discovered something wonderful—all the smells of Sam's kitchen. There had been a delightfully mixed aroma of apples, peanuts, bread, strong cheese, soup from a can, and, just faintly, there lingered a whiff of pizza.

Cato sighed. Tonight, when all the humans were asleep, he would climb out again. This time he would make sure he had a real feast.

## This Place Is Unsafe

Sam was working at his easel later in the morning when there was a knock at the door.

"Come in!" he shouted. Whoever was at the door knocked again.

"Botheration!" Sam wiped his hands on a piece of rag, strode over to the door, and opened it. A large man in a business suit stood on the doorstep.

"Mr. Fleming?" asked the man.

"Yes, I'm Sam Fleming."

"Brown is my name," the man said, holding out his hand. "I'm from the council. I'm the . . . er . . . building inspector."

Sam shook the man's hand and said, "You'd better come in." He stood back to let Mr. Brown walk past.

"You see . . . Mr. Fleming," said Mr. Brown, looking around, "we feel this cottage is unsafe. It could fall down at any time. It's not nice. In fact, it's a disgrace to this area. We have written to you a dozen times about it, but you've never answered. My council has decided that it must come down."

"Is that so? Well, in the first place, it's not a cottage. It's a studio."

"Well, whatever you call it, Mr. Fleming, we still think it's unsafe. Surely you would like to live in a better home?"

"My studio suits me just fine," Sam said. "Look at this, Mr. Brown." Sam moved over to the window. "I designed the studio so I could have this long window here. It goes all along the wall, you see. That's to let in plenty of light."

"Yes, well, er . . ." began Mr. Brown.

"And another thing—my bed is right here, so I am never far from my work. And another thing—the kitchen is small and handy so that I don't have to waste time when I want a bite to eat."

"Yes, handy, most handy." Mr. Brown stepped carefully around some canvases stacked on the floor.

"So you see, Mr. Brown, this isn't just an ordinary cottage. This is my studio, and it happens to be the only artist's studio in this town."

"Yes, I understand all that." Mr. Brown looked around for a place to sit, but all the chairs had brushes or tubes of paint on them. "I understand how you feel, but the whole trouble is that the building is not safe. It won't be much good as a studio if it all tumbles down around you, will it?"

Sam looked unhappy, but he didn't say anything.

"Now my suggestion, Mr. Fleming, is this. Build another . . . er . . . studio, just as good as this one. It can have a long window and everything else you need. But this time put up a solid building on your own piece of land. Get a builder to do it for you. Make it a good strong place that will last. Then the council will be quite happy."

"That sounds good," said Sam quietly. "But you've forgotten one thing. I'm an artist, not a millionaire. I haven't got the money to build a place like that."

"Well, it was just a suggestion," said Mr. Brown.

"Tell me one thing," Sam went on. "You say I've got to move, and if I don't, the council will pull this building, my studio—my home—down. How much time have I got?"

"Now, Mr. Fleming," Mr. Brown said, "we are only thinking of your safety. We won't pull it down for another two or three months. I think this cottage will stand for at least three more months, unless we get a hurricane or a cyclone—but that's most unlikely. Yes, you will certainly have three months."

# John Darcy's Brilliant Idea

Sam was walking out the side gate as John Darcy came home from school that afternoon.

"I'm on my way to the circus. Cato is still missing. I heard about it on the radio. Want to come with me?"

"Sure thing!" John said. "I'll just put my school bag inside and tell Mom."

The circus was not the happy place it had been. The performers just sat around or stood in sad little groups. No one was practicing. Even the animals seemed to feel something was wrong. They were all restless and even noisier than usual.

Mr. Borrill sat looking gloomy and depressed in the doorway of his trailer. His clothes were crumpled. His shoes were dusty.

"Good afternoon, Mr. Borrill. Any news?" Sam asked.

"Not a word."

"Didn't the police find any clues?" asked John.

"No, they didn't. Cato has disappeared without a trace. A lot of people came to the circus today just out of curiosity. They stood around saying things like, 'It's probably just a publicity stunt.' Of course, they didn't buy tickets for the circus. I tell you, Sam, without Cato I might as well not have a circus at all."

Stella came to the trailer door.

"Come on in. Let's all have a cup of tea," she said, looking from Sam to John. She was glad her father had company. It might make him feel better.

The four of them sat around the table in the trailer, drinking tea and eating chocolate cookies. In no time Sam found himself telling the Borrills about his own problems.

"Do you mean to say they can put you out of your own home?" asked Stella.

"Yes, it looks as though they can. They say it's not safe. I've got three months to find somewhere else to live."

"That's one problem I've never had," said Mr. Borrill. "I've always had my trailer. Say, that's an idea, Sam. Why not buy a trailer? It makes a very comfortable home."

"Mr. Borrill, I couldn't even buy a toy trailer. Artists don't make a lot of money, you know." Sam dunked his chocolate cookie. He kept it in his tea so long that the chocolate melted.

"But with your talent . . ." began Stella.

"Sam does make a lot of money," John said. "I know he does—but he doesn't know how to look after it. For one thing, he gives it away."

"Do you mean he wastes it?" asked Mr. Borrill.

"No, it's not wasted," John answered. "I mean, there was the time I wanted a microscope. Mom couldn't afford to get me one, so Sam bought one for me. Not a cheap one, either. It was a really good one. He sent away to the city for it."

Stella smiled at Sam.

"Then there was the time he found out that a boy in my class had never been to the beach. Sam gave the boy's mother a bus ticket and arranged for him to stay with a family. Then there was the time —"

"Enough!" Sam said. "Not another word." He took a big mouthful of his chocolate-flavored tea. "Stella, this is the best tea I've ever tasted. Now, let's change the subject. Le Vram, that magician, was in a towering rage yesterday after the matinee show. What's become of him?"

"Huh, Le Vram! I'll tell you about him." Mr. Borrill told of their quarrel, Le Vram's jealousy, and the magician's threat to ruin the circus.

"He's left the circus. He stamped out of my trailer and I haven't seen him since. I've been too worried about Cato to waste much time thinking about jealous magicians. If he does show up again, I certainly won't hire him. As far as I'm concerned, he's finished with the circus forever."

"I hear they've had a lot of terrible thunderstorms along the highway and at some little town in the mountains," Stella said. She looked puzzled. "Now why on earth would I say a thing like that, when we weren't even talking about the weather? We were talking about that nasty magician. I tell you, Father, I never liked him very much. I didn't want you to hire him in the first place. I thought he looked evil."

When it was time to go, Sam said to Mr. Borrill, "I know your elephant will turn up. Elephants never get lost. He's probably gone for a short holiday all by himself. He'll be found. Don't you worry anymore. Well, we have to get home."

As they walked through the quiet circus grounds, John felt sad. He wondered if he would ever see the circus people again.

All the way home he was quiet. Sam spoke to him a couple of times but he did not answer. He was thinking.

At home John found his mother in the kitchen.

"Well, John," she said, "I've been baking all day. I've made a lot of cupcakes for the Hospital Aid Society's street fair tomorrow. But I've saved some for you."

John said, "Oh hello, Mom," and walked through the kitchen.

*Well,* thought Mrs. Darcy, *he* must *have something on his mind. I've never seen him turn down a cupcake before.*

Later John wandered over to the studio. Sam was sitting at a table, sketching. A plate of stew was untouched beside him.

John roamed around the studio for a while, looking at Sam's work. His favorite painting was one called *Trapeze Artists.* It showed two trapeze fliers, a man and a woman, performing on a high swing. Actually, the people in the picture were quite small. The tightly stretched canvas of the big top arched above them. Below them, small and far away, John could see the crowd—blurred—as the trapeze artists would have seen them if they had glanced down during their dizzying flight. The trapeze fliers looked tiny and alone in that vast space, as though all they had to depend on was each other—which was true. The man had just spun in a somersault and was about to clutch the woman's outstretched hands. Although the woman was small, her hands appeared large, strong, and dependable.

"Your paintings look so alive, Sam," John said. After a while he added, "You've got a lot of pictures, haven't you?"

"Hmmm . . ."

"There must be dozens."

"Quite a few," Sam said.

"Sam, listen to me. I've got a great idea."

Sam looked up from his sketch.

"You need money. Right?"

"Right."

"And you're an artist. Right?"

"Right."

"Well, I know a way for you to earn money, Sam. Have a show!"

"A show!"

"Yes—an art show. Put all your paintings in it. Invite people to come. They can pay to come in, then they can buy the paintings. That way you'll sell them all, and you'll have enough money to build yourself a brand-new studio. Or you could buy a trailer. Isn't that a great idea?"

Sam sprang to his feet. "You're right!" he cried.

He raced around the studio, picking up paintings and drawings and looking at them.

"Here we are: sad clowns, happy clowns, angry lions, shy lions, brilliant sunsets, stormy skies. Dozens more. Dozens! You're right, John, that's exactly what I'll do. I'll have a show. Then I won't have to worry what the council does about this studio."

# In the Newspaper Again

A week later, John went over to the studio. "We have to do some planning, Sam," he said.

"Planning for what?" Sam was sitting by the long window, looking across the street at the movie theater. A line of people waited at the box office.

"For the art show, of course," said John.

"The show. Oh, yes, I remember," said Sam, turning away from the window. "But what could there possibly be to do? All we have to do is hang up the paintings, then tell everyone to come and look at them."

"It's not as easy as that, Sam. I've been talking to Mom. She's organized lots of things like this. You know, she's on the Children's Home Committee and she's in the Hospital Aid Society and the Garden Club and the Discussion Group—"

"I know, I know—she's in everything," Sam cut in. "You're right. If there's anyone who knows about organizing things, it's your mom. What does she think we should do first?"

"Well, we have to hire a hall, have the tickets printed, make posters to put in store windows, and a dozen other things."

Suddenly John stopped. "Ssh," he whispered. "Sam, I thought I heard something in the kitchen. I bet you've got mice."

"Well, if I have, just leave them alone," said Sam. "The poor things will soon be like me—nowhere to live. Let them enjoy themselves while they've got a home."

Sam spent the next two weeks finishing his paintings.

One morning there was a knock at the door. Mrs. Darcy came in, carrying a bundle of letters in one hand and a newspaper in the other. "Here's your mail, Sam," she said. "I'll put it on the counter top for you."

She dropped the bundle of letters onto the counter. "Sam, did you know your wallet's here? You're going to lose everything out of it if you leave it lying around like this."

"Don't worry about it," Sam said.

"Did you hear that the circus has left town?" Mrs. Darcy asked, as she sat on the edge of the table.

"Yes, I heard. I hope they come back soon."

"And that's not all," his sister said. "Here's this morning's paper. What do you think of this piece of news?"

Taking the newspaper, Sam looked at the story that she was pointing to and read it aloud.

### REWARD FOR ELEPHANT

So far no trace has been found of Cato, the elephant that disappeared mysteriously from Borrill's Circus while it was in town three weeks ago.

The well-known city businessman, Reginald Bisk, has offered a reward of $1000 to anyone who gives information leading to the finding of Cato.

Mr. Bisk, reported to be a millionaire, has taken a keen interest in entertainment and circuses over the years. He owns several theaters and has often sponsored special performances. He told newspaper reporters that he hoped the offer of reward money would help to locate the missing elephant . . .

"Reginald Bisk! I've heard of him." Sam sounded excited. "He's the man who arranges Christmas shows every year in the city."

He read the newspaper story again. "One thousand dollars. I could do a lot with a thousand dollars. I'd like to be the one to find Cato. It's not only for the money, though. I'd hate to see Mr. Borrill and Stella having to close down their circus."

"I think that elephant has been stolen, Sam," said his sister. "I think that someone in this town has that elephant hidden away in his garage."

"But why would anyone want to keep an elephant in a garage?"

"Well, I've never been able to figure out why people do some of the things they do. That's my opinion anyway. Someone has hidden the elephant away. How on earth they are managing to feed it and keep it hidden, I wouldn't know."

"No, Annie, I disagree. Nobody would be that mean," Sam said. "Just wait. I wouldn't be surprised if that elephant turned up suddenly one day right here in town."

"Well, I must go now," Mrs. Darcy said. "It's the meeting of the Children's Home Committee today, and I think this meeting will be a long one. The Children's Home badly needs a swimming pool, and we are trying to raise the money to build one. You know how hot it gets here in the summertime. Good-bye, Sam."

When she had gone, Sam put down his brushes and thought for a while. He thought about the circus and Stella. He thought about Cato and the thousand dollars. Then he wondered where he was going to live when his studio was pulled down. John seemed to think that the art show was the answer to all Sam's problems.

But it seemed to Sam that the answer to everything was Cato. He didn't know why, but it seemed to him that if Cato could be found, everything would be all right.

Meanwhile, Le Vram was sitting on the front porch of his cottage up in the mountains. He was reading the newspaper story about Reginald Bisk's reward.

He laughed to himself as he read. "I've really

got them baffled this time. That's what magic is all about—baffling. If the audience is not baffled, then the magician isn't any good."

Then he cut out the story and carefully pasted it in his scrapbook. He was collecting reports about Cato's disappearance from every newspaper or magazine he saw.

He still could not remember the formula he had used to make Cato disappear. Every day he studied his books of magic or searched through his many notebooks. He found every formula and spell a magician could ever need, but none of them seemed to be the correct one. Nevertheless, he knew that, for once, he had performed a spectacular trick.

# The Discovery of Peanut Butter

Cato was taking his morning nap when Mrs. Darcy dropped the mail onto the counter top. He opened his eyes as he heard the letters flop above him. One of them dropped through the hole. He placed it on top of the pile of other letters stacked in the corner.

He walked around in his drawer wondering if there was anything to eat and listening to Mrs. Darcy talk to Sam.

He felt a little pang when he heard her say that the circus had left town. They've gone— without me, he thought. He wondered if he would ever see the circus again.

Cato was missing the fun of circus life. He longed for the shouts and noise and music and laughter. Most of all, he missed the applause.

All his life, people had been clapping and cheering for him—and now there was nobody to do it.

In the weeks he had been living in Sam's kitchen, he had learned to do some very clever things, such as walking along the edge of the kitchen sink, dropping the plug into the hole so that water from the dripping tap would make a pool for him to bathe in, and carrying bundles of food down the sloping board into the drawer.

He felt proud of these things, and every time he did something clever he expected to hear clapping—but he heard nothing. Nobody clapped. Nobody cheered. No children placed their warm, sticky hands on his trunk. Nobody fed him peanuts or buns or apples.

He remembered the time when a little boy had liked him so much that he had tried to persuade his father to buy him and take him home. He remembered the times he had heard Mr. Borrill say, "Cato is the star of this show." They were very happy memories.

Sam was reading from a newspaper, and Cato heard him say, ". . . offered a reward of one thousand dollars . . ."

One thousand dollars! Cato knew that one thousand dollars must be a large amount of money. Imagine anyone wanting to pay that much for him—he must be quite valuable.

That night a bright full moon sent a silvery glow into the little kitchen of Sam's studio. When all was quiet, Cato set out to explore some more.

The first thing he did was climb down the drainer, slide the plug into its hole, and have a bath. He loved water. He loved the refreshing, clean feeling it gave him. He lifted his trunk and let the cool trickles run down his back.

After his bath, he went looking for things to eat. Since he had come to live in the kitchen drawer, Cato had tasted some interesting new foods. He had nibbled at an apple pie, he had drunk some milk, he had tasted cold coffee, he had eaten cold french fries, and even a whole tomato sandwich.

Now he noticed some things that looked like green trees cut down and piled on top of each other. Cato broke off one of the leaves and tasted it. It had a crisp, cool, greenish taste.

It was celery. With utter enjoyment Cato
crunched and munched at the celery. Then he
noticed a familiar smell; it reminded him of

the circus. He lifted his trunk and sniffed. Peanuts! But where was it coming from? There was not a peanut in sight.

He followed the smell to an open jar that stood beside the bunch of celery. Cato raised his trunk and placed it over the top of the jar, expecting to take out a few peanuts. To his surprise he scooped up a trunkful of buttery goo—but the taste was exactly like peanuts!

What a good meal, he thought, green leaves and peanuts. After a while he felt pleasantly full, so full that he felt like sending out a great, loud, trumpeting roar. He lifted his trunk, opened his mouth, and . . . squeaked—the silliest, softest, littlest squeak ever made by any circus animal.

I can't even trumpet anymore, thought Cato sadly. Still, he felt good after his bath and meal. He broke off a branch of the celery and held it in his trunk like a flag. He made his way across the cupboard, carefully stepped through the hole onto his board, and returned to his home.

# The Meeting of Old Friends

Sam soon found out that John and Mrs. Darcy had been right. Holding an art show did take a lot of planning and work.

While Sam was finishing and framing his pictures, John had posters made and went around town asking storekeepers to place them in their windows. Most important, he hired the School of Arts hall for the show.

The weather grew hotter. The sun stood high in the sky like a red-hot plate, and the little town cooked under its heat.

People walked around town mopping their brows and saying, "Looks as though we're in for a hot summer. Very hot."

The ground felt hard and dry underfoot. The trees and shrubs growing in the gardens began to droop, and the old people sat on their porches in the shade, fanning themselves.

John Darcy came home from school and ran into the yard, where Sam was making picture frames.

"Guess what!" John said. "I've just put the last of the posters in the bookstore window."

"Great," said Sam. He was not as excited as John had expected.

"I thought you'd be jumping for joy, Sam," he said.

"Well, I would be—except that I've just had a visit from our friend the councilman, Mr. Brown."

"And what did he want?"

"He came to tell me to move out next month. He said that it's nearly two months since he first came to see me, and I'm still living here. They're going to pull my studio down. It looks like I'll have to move into your spare room."

"That's tough," John said.

"Oh, I suppose it's not as bad as all that." Sam brightened up a little as he looked at his picture frames. "Soon I'll have enough money to get another studio. This art show is going to be a big success."

"You bet it is."

Sam gathered up his wood, tacks, saw, and hammer. "I've done enough work for today. Let's go down and take another look at that School of Arts hall."

By the time Sam and John got there the hall was closed, so they walked around outside looking through the windows.

"We'll come down here the day before and hang all the pictures," Sam said.

"I've already arranged for that," John answered. "And I've asked if we can have one of our posters put up outside, on this wall here, so that people walking past will know that the art show is going to be on."

The sun was setting. Long shadows stretched across the ground, and the leaves in the trees began to shake and rustle in the cool evening breeze.

"Let's walk back through town. I want to buy some supper," Sam said.

They walked slowly, stopping to talk to people. Sam knew just about everyone in town. Most people were on their way home from work, and a few were out for an evening walk. Everyone wanted to enjoy the breeze.

By the time they arrived at their own street, it was almost dark. Although the movie theater was still closed, a few people were gathering outside, waiting for the box office to open.

"I wonder what's on tonight," said John, stopping outside the theater. As he looked through the glass door, he could see a man inside the theater—a fat man wearing a plaid vest and a gold watch chain.

"Sam!" John cried. "Sam, there's someone we know in there. Look, it's Mr. Borrill."

At that moment the door flew open, and Mr. Borrill rushed out.

"Sam! John! My old friends. How good to see you."

He clutched Sam's right hand with his own right hand, and, wanting to shake hands with John too, grabbed John's left hand with his left. He stood there shaking their hands and saying, "I've been looking for you two ever since we came to town. I was wondering when I'd see you."

"What are you doing here?" asked Sam, still shaking Mr. Borrill's hand. "Where's the circus? In the same place again?"

Mr. Borrill let go of their hands. "There's no circus now. We've given it up. Nobody would come to the circus, so we sold out and moved here. We are managing this movie theater now."

"So Stella's here too?" asked Sam.

"She's inside the theater right now. She'll be glad to see you two." He turned and stepped inside the doorway. "Stella. Stella, come and see who's here."

Stella opened the glass door and came out.

"Sam, John—what a surprise." Stella laughed and shook hands with them both. "We've been looking for you two ever since we came back to town."

"I've already told them that," said Mr. Borrill, laughing. "Isn't it good to see old friends?"

More people had gathered outside the theater. They had formed a line and were looking quite impatient. Mr. Borrill said, "It looks as though we'll have to open up."

"Look, Mr. Borrill, Stella," Sam said. "I won't keep you now. But I live just across the road. See that building over there with the long window? That's my studio. Come and visit me tonight after the show. **We can have some** coffee and a long talk."

"We certainly will," said Stella.

"Yes, indeed we will," Mr. Borrill joined in. "Right after the show, we'll be over."

With a smile Stella turned and went into the box office. She waved to John and Sam and began selling tickets.

# Animal Tracks

"I'm having visitors!" cried Sam, rushing into the studio. "I'm having visitors!"

"Calm down, Sam." John followed Sam inside. "You often have visitors."

"Yes, but these are special." Sam began rushing around, moving things from one place to another. "I'll have to clean up. They'll need somewhere to sit. Coffee! I'll make coffee. Have I got any cookies?"

John carefully gathered up the coffee cups. There were two under the bed and two more on the windowsill. He dodged Sam who was dashing around making things worse.

All together John found eight coffee cups. Some still had cold coffee in them, and some held paintbrushes or drawing charcoal. He took them all into the kitchen, emptied them, and stacked them in the sink.

Meanwhile, Sam tipped up all the chairs and dumped everything that had been on them onto the middle of the coffee table. Paper, pencils, and paint-splotched ice-cream container lids spilled onto the floor.

In the kitchen John checked to see whether Sam had enough coffee, sugar, and milk.

"You don't seem to have any milk left, Sam," he called, peering into Sam's little refrigerator.

"No milk? I thought I had plenty. What will I do?" Sam called from inside the studio.

"There must be a store still open, maybe the corner market."

"Good idea. I'll go out and buy some. Money!" Sam slapped his pockets. "None on me. Where's my wallet?"

He found the wallet in its usual place on the counter top. It lay opened with money spilling out. Sam picked it up and jammed it into his pocket.

"I'll get some crackers, too, and some cheese." He raced out, banging the door behind him.

When Sam had gone, John began to look around for food for supper.

On the kitchen table he found a package of cookies. It had been torn open, and some of the cookies had been taken out—but they had not all been eaten. Beside the cookies lay a pile of cherries, but only half of each cherry was there.

He found a peanut butter jar on the table, beside a half-eaten apple. The jar lay on its side with peanut butter spilling out. As John stood the jar up, he noticed tiny peanut-buttery animal tracks going across the table.

John leaned over close to the table, peering through his glasses. The tracks went to the end of the table, then onto the sink. There they were almost washed away by water. Onward they went, however, across the back of the sink and onto the counter. At this point the tracks had almost disappeared, and only a trace of peanut butter could be seen. John bent closer. The tracks seemed to go right up to the hole in the counter top.

He moved back to the table where the tracks were still quite clear. He tried to think of what kind of animal had made them. They were not mouse tracks, but they certainly had been made by a four-footed creature. He tried to imagine what kind of tiny animal could get into Sam's kitchen. He thought of possums, lizards, even kittens—but the tracks could not possibly belong to any of these.

He went back to the cupboard. He heard a faint scuffle, a rustling of paper, inside the drawer. As he had done once before, he tried to pull the drawer open, but it was still stuck fast. He leaned closer, trying to look through the hole. It was too dark inside the drawer. He couldn't see anything.

John heard a sound at the door. His mother walked in, carrying a cake.

"I thought I'd find you here," she said. She put the cake down beside the peanut butter jar. "Where's Sam?"

"He's just gone out to buy some milk. He's having visitors tonight after the movies. Remember Mr. Borrill and Stella from the circus? They're living here now, and they're coming for coffee tonight."

"Well, it's a good thing I brought this cake for Sam," Mrs. Darcy said. "It was left over from the Children's Home cake sale. I thought Sam could use it."

John told his mother all about how Mr. Borrill and Stella had given up the circus and were now managing the movie theater. While she listened, Mrs. Darcy looked around the kitchen.

"He's having visitors? Just look at this mess. Half-eaten cookies, peanut butter spilled everywhere. This will have to be cleaned up."

She rushed around putting things away. John helped but kept looking back at that closed cupboard drawer. Something there— something was living in that drawer.

## If Ye Be Angry Enough

"So there is still no clue as to where your elephant is, Mr. Borrill?" asked Mrs. Darcy.

"No clue. The police have looked into it thoroughly. Reginald Bisk has offered a big reward. We have spent a fortune advertising in all the papers. But there's been no answer. Cato, the star of our circus, seems to have vanished from the face of the earth."

"That's terrible—and it's so mysterious." Mrs. Darcy sounded very sympathetic.

"The trouble was," Mr. Borrill went on, "that I had sent people ahead to all the towns to paste up Sam's posters. Cato was so popular that everyone wanted to see him. When the circus arrived in town with no Cato, the people called me a fraud. Audiences were so small that I couldn't afford to pay my workers."

"Don't be gloomy anymore, Father," said Stella. She was wandering around the studio admiring Sam's pictures. She walked back over to the chair where her father was sitting. "At least we have friends, and you always did like this little town."

Five people were in Sam's studio. Mrs. Darcy was sitting beside Mr. Borrill, listening to the story of how his circus was lost. Sam was standing beside Stella, showing her his latest paintings and listening to her tell the misfortunes of Borrill's Circus. John was crouching on the floor near the big window. He was searching through a pile of encyclopedias and other books, and beside him on the floor lay a flashlight.

"Father, let's forget about circus problems for a while," Stella said. "Did you know that Sam is planning an art show?"

"Yes, so I heard. Tell us all about it, Sam."

Sam sat on the floor and stretched his long legs out in front of him. He told Mr. Borrill and Stella about the show, and how he planned to make enough money to get a new studio.

"As a matter of fact, Mr. Borrill," he went on, "I've thought a lot about your idea of buying a trailer. If I could get enough money, that's what I'd like to do. I'd buy a trailer and travel around the country painting landscapes. Out beyond the mountains I believe there's some beautiful country to paint—mysterious light and shade in the mornings, eerie shadows in the evenings."

John hardly heard the conversation around him. He had found what he wanted in the encyclopedia. He looked up slowly, with his mouth open. He sat for a long time gazing through Sam's long window. Outside, there was darkness with a few pinpoints of light. His finger was still on the open page, at the very place where he had found the information. It was a drawing of the tracks of various jungle animals. John's finger was pointing to the picture of elephant tracks.

His mind whirred away like a computer. Those round pools of water—they had been animal tracks. And the marks in the peanut butter. He could not believe it!

Slowly and quietly, while the others talked, he stood up and picked up his flashlight. He slipped into the kitchen and closed the door behind him.

He looked at the cupboard counter and at the jumble of things on top of it. He stood absolutely still for a moment. Then he switched on the flashlight but kept his hand over its beam. Slowly he tiptoed toward the cupboard. With a sudden movement he leaned over and pointed the flashlight through the hole.

Nothing! There seemed to be some papers there—and something shiny, perhaps a coin— but it was too dark inside, and the hole was too small, to make out anything else. A piece of paper could be seen in the dim glow of the flashlight as he moved it back and forth.

John switched off the light and walked back to the studio. Again he sat on the floor with books scattered around him.

". . . very mean of the council, but in a way, I can't help agreeing with them . . ." Mrs. Darcy was saying, while Sam poured more coffee.

John hardly heard or noticed. He was too busy. "If it can't be explained by science, perhaps it can be explained by something else," he said to himself, picking up another book. It was a huge volume called *Centuries of Sorcery and Magic*. As John flipped through it, he saw pictures of witches, hobgoblins, unicorns, and creatures with shimmering wings.

The chapters had headings such as "Alchemy," "Use of Herbs and Plants," "Astrology and the Power of the Heavens," and "Foretelling the Future."

At the beginning of each chapter was a picture. One was of glass bottles and tubes with colored vapors coming out of them. Another was of plants in the shape of people. Another was of the stars and the moon. And another was a picture of a crystal ball.

Nearly every second page showed a picture of ancient documents. They were yellowed and torn, and the writing was barely readable. One told how to create storms at sea, and another told how to turn milk sour "with no touching by hand."

There were curses like "How to make your enemy's ears turn green."

There were spells like "Place two drops of this potion into a person's eyes and he shall fall in love with whoever he looks upon."

There were recipes like "To make warts go away, take a toenail, whiskers of three rats . . ."

There were chemical formulas like "To make pure gold from iron."

Every possible use of magic was listed in the book, but one particular document caught John's attention. The printing was hard to read, but he made out these words:

To All Ye
who would do
MAGICK
Worke and study welle
and ye shall do all manner
of wonders.

Great things can be made small
and lyttle things made large
and fair maides changed
into toades

if ye be
Angry Enough!

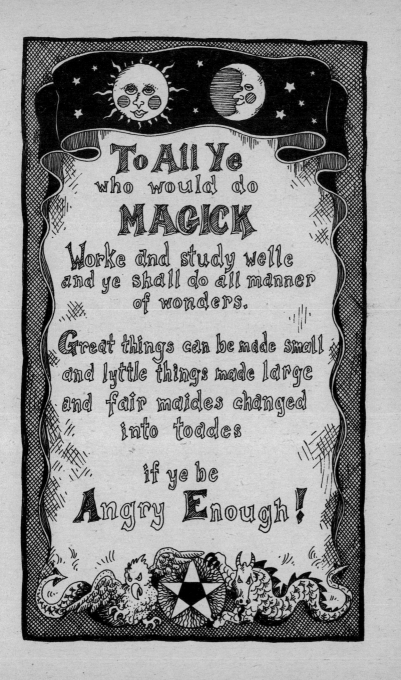

"Impossible," John said to himself. And yet—a magician had been very angry, an elephant was a "great thing," and in Sam's kitchen there was a very "little thing."

"Impossible," John said again—but he still wondered.

# Meeting a Millionaire

The School of Arts had never been busier nor looked brighter than it did on the day of Sam Fleming's art show.

Sam, John, and Stella had planned and organized for weeks. In the final week they decorated the hall and hung the pictures. Every picture was numbered, and John and Stella had printed lists of the paintings so people would know the title of each one. Besides the paintings, there were sketches done with pencil and charcoal, and tiny pictures painted with water colors.

Because the School of Arts was on the main street, people popped in and out all day. Sam wandered around, so tall that his bushy beard seemed to float above the heads of the crowd.

He talked to people and shook hundreds of hands. Everyone wanted to meet the artist.

It seemed that everyone wanted to buy a Sam Fleming painting. The principal of John's school bought a landscape to hang in the school assembly hall. The hospital bought a circus painting to hang in the children's ward. The Children's Home Committee did not buy a picture, though. They were saving all their money for the swimming pool.

In the middle of the afternoon, John was helping Stella count some money when a little man wearing a shabby suit approached him. John had noticed this man earlier. He had been at the show for an hour or two and had stood for a long time in front of every picture.

"I'd like to meet the artist," the man said to John. "You seem to be organizing things here; what about taking me over and introducing me to Sam Fleming?"

"Yes, come with me," John said.

"Bisk is my name," the man said as they walked over to Sam.

Sam was standing in a corner, talking to a woman who held a notebook in her hand. She was tall and thin, her hair was a startling pink, and she wore sunglasses almost big enough to cover her whole face.

"Hello there, John," said Sam. "This is Marjorie from the local newspaper. She says she is going to write an article about the show for the next issue."

"I certainly am. This is one of the greatest cultural events this town has ever had. To think that we have a real artist living here in our little town. . . ."

"Ahem." The man standing beside John cleared his throat.

"Oh, yes, er . . ." John began. "Sam, and Marjorie, this is Mr. Bisk."

*Bisk*, thought Sam, *Bisk*. He had heard that name, but could not remember where.

"Reginald Bisk," announced the little man, shaking hands with Sam and bowing to Marjorie.

"Oh, yes!" Sam said. "Now I remember. Reginald Bisk—you're the man who offered a reward for Cato."

"That's right," said Mr. Bisk. He turned to John. "And are you the artist's brother?"

"No, nephew," John answered. "Sam is my uncle."

"I dabble in a lot of things, as you probably know," Mr. Bisk said to the three of them. "I'm a businessman actually, but I'm interested in many other things. Now—I happen to be opening an art gallery in the city. You know I'm interested in the circus. Most interested. I've just bought some of the pictures for my gallery."

"He looked at *all* the circus pictures," John told Sam.

"Yes, indeed I did. They are very fine examples. Now, Mr. Fleming, I'm interested in your work. Here's my card. I'll be coming to this town from time to time and I'll arrange to see you. I want to see all your work because I'm anxious to show it and sell it in the city."

"Yes. Thank you. Thank you." Sam took the card.

"Any news of the missing elephant?" John asked Mr. Bisk.

"Nothing positive, just rumors. For example, a farmer thirty miles from here called the police one night and told them to get out to his place and bring the reward money because he could see the elephant from his window.

When the police got there (without the reward money, of course) they found that there was no elephant. The man had been looking at one of his own haystacks in the moonlight."

John, Sam, and Marjorie all laughed at Mr. Bisk's story.

"Oh, yes," he went on, "that elephant has been blamed for just about everything. It's, let me see, nearly three months since he disappered. If fruit is stolen from trees, the owner thinks Cato did it. If someone a hundred miles in the opposite direction hears noises in the night, he telephones the police and reports he's found the missing elephant. By the way, I've met Mr. Borrill. Wonderful man. In my opinion circus people bring a great deal of joy and happiness to the world."

All afternoon and evening people came to the art show. All of Sam's friends wanted to buy pictures, and people he did not know wanted to meet him because they believed he must be famous. He shook hands so often that he thought his fingers would be too stiff to hold a paintbrush ever again.

Late that night the same five people were

seated once again in Sam's studio. The heat of the day had been chased away by a cool breeze. Through the studio window the lights of the little town could be seen against the dark sky.

After the excitement and hard work of the day, no one felt very much like talking. They sipped their coffee and rested.

Sam said, almost to himself, "Every picture was sold. Every one."

"Reginald Bisk doesn't look much like a millionaire," Mr. Borrill said.

"He thinks we should get the circus back on the road somehow—with or without Cato," Stella said.

John's thoughts weren't on the circus at all. "By the time we've finished counting the money," he said, "you should have enough for that trailer, Sam."

Mrs. Darcy added, "I think you'll need that trailer soon, Sam. I can feel that wind blowing right through the cracks in these walls."

Sam sat up with a look of surprise. "You know, you're right, Annie. This studio *will* fall down soon. Just look at the cracks in the walls.

It's a good thing I'm moving out tomorrow."

Mr. Borrill stood up and yawned. "Do you think we should be going, Stella?"

"Yes, Father. It's been a long day. Good night, Sam. We'll come and visit again soon."

"Yes, come on, John—it's time for us to go, too," said Mrs. Darcy. She and John stood up and started walking toward the door.

On the way out, John glanced over at the counter top. Earlier that day he had placed a lettuce leaf and two peanuts beside the hole. They were gone.

# Sam's Big Decision

Sam opened his eyes and blinked at the bright sunlight shining through the window. Someone was knocking at the door.

"Hold on, hold on. I'm coming!" he called. Half asleep, he stumbled across the room and opened the door.

"What's all the noise?" he asked when he saw John Darcy.

"It's nine o'clock. You asked me to wake you early this morning, remember? Today is the day when you have to move all your things out. Mom's cleared the spare room. You can't stay in bed."

"It's already too hot to work," Sam said.

"I know it is, but Mom says you have to move today. Tomorrow the wreckers are coming."

When they carried the first loaded card-board cartons into Mrs. Darcy's kitchen, they found her taking pans of cookies out of the oven.

She looked so unhappy that Sam stopped and said, "What's up, Annie? Something wrong?"

Mrs. Darcy mopped her brow with her apron. "There certainly is something wrong," she answered. "Our town council makes me mad. Here it is, a sweltering day, and I'm in this hot kitchen making cookies."

"Well, you can't blame the council for the weather, Annie."

"No, but it's their fault I'm making cookies," she snapped. "These cookies are for sale. The other ladies are making them too. We're going to put them in packages and sell them. They're to raise money for the swimming pool for the Children's Home."

She put another panful of cookies into the oven and shut the door.

"That's why this council makes me mad! They should give us a swimming pool. It's ri-diculous that in a place that gets as hot as this, there's not even a town pool where people can swim. And look at the way they're turning you out of your home without giving you somewhere else to live."

"Never mind, Mom," John said. "The Children's Home is sure to get its pool someday. With all the work you and your committee have done, you must have raised a lot of money."

"Yes, 'someday' is right." His mother measured more flour into her mixing bowl. "A decent swimming pool costs a great deal, and we won't have enough money this year. It looks as though the children will have to wait until next year for their pool."

She cut off a hunk of butter and dropped it into the bowlful of flour. She looked up and smiled at Sam and John. "I'm sorry I sounded so angry. I shouldn't be worrying you two with all this. Here, have some cookies. They're fresh and hot."

By mid-afternoon, Sam had moved a lot of his things. The bed, the table, and the chairs were still in place, but they were no longer covered with clutter. The studio looked bare and deserted, and Sam felt uncomfortable in such a tidy place.

The kitchen had not been touched. The sink, the table, and the cupboard were all as they had been. Sam had decided to move everything out of there last.

As Sam stood in the middle of the studio looking around sadly, Mr. Borrill appeared at the open door.

"Come in," said Sam. Mr. Borrill walked in and sat down on Sam's bed. He opened a small suitcase.

"Well, here it is. Stella has spent all morning counting your money and sorting it into bundles. Here is all the cash, and here are the checks. This is a list of the paintings showing how much they were sold for. Stella is very careful when it comes to business matters."

Sam stared at the bundles of money neatly stacked in the suitcase. "Good heavens, I must be a millionaire!" he said.

"Not quite," answered Mr. Borrill, "but we could say you are a successful artist. With this money you could buy yourself a nice little trailer."

"Just what I've been wanting," Sam said.

"The best thing about all this, though, Sam, is that Reginald Bisk said he will sell your paintings in his gallery from now on. Sam, you need never be a poor, struggling artist again."

Sam sat down and looked at the money. He had never dreamed that he could earn so much by doing what he loved—painting.

"There's only one place for this," said Mr. Borrill, "and that's the bank. I suggest that you put it in the bank right away."

"Yes, I'll go now," said Sam, standing up. "You come with me, Mr. Borrill. I'll put the money in the bank, and get a checkbook. Then I can get money any time I want, simply by writing a check."

Late that afternoon, Sam hummed happily as he fussed around in the studio kitchen making his supper. His new checkbook was in his pocket and he had hundreds of dollars in the bank. He could buy anything he wanted—well, almost anything. He wasn't as rich as Reginald Bisk. He wasn't really rich at all. He was simply an artist who had finally managed to earn some money.

As his sausages cooked, he made plans. He would buy a trailer. He would take sketch books, some pencils and charcoal and paints—then off he would go. He would travel around the country seeing things he had never seen before, and everywhere he went he would paint and draw. The best plan of all was that he was going to ask Stella to marry him.

He put the sausages on a plate and made himself a mug of coffee.

It was a warm night. As Sam sipped his coffee, he grew warmer. Right now, he thought, it would be pleasant to go for a swim and cool off. Annie's right. It is ridiculous that the town has no swimming pool. He thought of the children at the Children's Home, and how much they needed a pool of their own.

He stood up and walked over to the window. For a long time he stood there, thinking.

*This is probably my last night in this studio, my very own home. It's strange how important it is to have a home.* He thought of the children again. Many of them had been homeless at some time in their lives. Some of them had no parents.

He thought of Mr. Borrill and Stella. Every year they had given the children from the Children's Home free seats at the circus, but now there was no circus for them to go to.

Sam could see the lights of houses winking and blinking in the night. "I'm a good artist," he said to himself. "I don't really need to travel around in a trailer. I can stay right here, living in Annie's spare room. I can earn more money with my paintings—Mr. Bisk said so."

He went to the kitchen and searched around till he found a pen. Then he took the new checkbook out of his pocket. He wrote a check to the Children's Home. It was for all the money he had in his bank account. Across the bottom of the check, he wrote: "For the swimming pool."

Sam went back to the window and stood there for a long time, thinking. He thought about the laughter of children at the circus, of the happiness of children swimming, of Reginald Bisk talking about the joy that circus people bring. He thought about Stella, and he knew that she would be proud of what he had done.

He was so full of his thoughts that he didn't notice that one of John's library books, *Centuries of Sorcery and Magic,* was lying open on a chair. If Sam had noticed it, he would have seen that it was open at a page that John meant to show him. The page looked very old. The words which John had read, but which Sam did not see, were:

Heed my warning: These Magicks, these curses, however powerful, are for Evil. Lette not any personne do goode, nor be kinde, nor give happyness to another. For truely this will end the Magick. If ye would bed true sorcerer, carry no kind thought in your heart. For then Magick cannot live.

Sam didn't know about the warning. And he didn't know that in a drawer in his kitchen cupboard, a tiny elephant moved—and began to feel cramped in that small space. The elephant stretched in his sleep and, for a moment, felt a strange warm glow.

## Sam's Party

The next morning Sam got up early. The sun streamed through the window on the peeling paint and cracked walls of his studio.

"It's a wonder this studio is still standing," he said to himself. "I've always been too busy to notice how bad it was before."

Sam still had some packing to do. His bed, table, and chairs were still in the studio. The little kitchen had not been touched.

He stood in the kitchen looking around. He liked his kitchen. He thought the shoes and brushes and papers scattered all over the counter top gave it a cozy look. He felt sad at leaving it. He had to find something to cheer himself up.

Suddenly he had a great idea. The wreckers had changed their plans. They weren't coming until tomorrow. He would hold a party to-night—a moving-out party! He would use up all the food and drinks he could find, and he would ask everybody to come.

There were plenty of people he could invite—John, Annie, Stella and her father. He would even ask Mr. Brown, the councilman, to show there were no hard feelings—and Marjorie from the newspaper. He wondered whether Reginald Bisk was still in town. Then there were all his other friends, dozens of them. Sam didn't even think about whether they could all fit into his studio, he just hoped they would all come.

He spent the day on his party plans. John went with him all over town, inviting friends. "It's a moving-out party," Sam told them all.

By late afternoon everyone had said they would come. Stella found someone to look after the movie theater so that she and her father could have the night off.

As John stood at Sam's sink, washing glasses, he said, "Sam, you're never going to fit everyone in the studio. Where will you put them all?"

"They'll all fit in somehow, don't worry," Sam answered.

Mrs. Darcy appeared in the doorway. "Here you are, Sam, I've brought a dozen glasses, in case you need them. Now I want you to come over and see how I've arranged the furniture in your new room."

"All right. Come to think of it, I need to rest before everyone gets here. Let's sit a minute."

Sam, Mrs. Darcy, and John walked out of the kitchen.

## Danger in the Kitchen

In the three months Cato had lived in Sam's kitchen he had become very clever. He had learned to tiptoe around on the table. He knew how to hide behind cups so he could see and hear what was happening. Now he was worried. He had heard enough to know he would not have a home much longer.

He had seen Mr. Borrill and Stella visiting Sam, and he had heard them talking about him. He wished he could climb down off the kitchen cupboard and give a loud trumpeting call. He could just imagine how happy Mr. Borrill's face would be when he saw his missing elephant. But this was impossible. Cato was only a few inches high, and all he could manage was a squeak.

Anyway, elephants cannot climb. Cato was

built for crashing through jungles. He could lift and pull. He could balance on tiny stools in the circus ring. He could walk on a board. There were lots of things he *could* do, but no matter what happened he would never be able to climb down from the kitchen cupboard. He could not jump either. When the time came for him to leave, he would have to find some other way of getting down.

Inside Sam's cupboard drawer he had made a very comfortable home. His bed was in one corner. In another corner, he had a large stack of Sam's unopened mail, which had slipped through the hole. Beside this, he had piles and piles of pieces of colored paper with pictures and numbers on them. Most of them had been in the drawer when he arrived. They had probably been slipping through the hole for years. They were green, black, and white. Some of them were crumpled and quite old.

He also had coins which had fallen out of Sam's wallet. Cato had stacked these, and they were just like the stools and drums he had stood on in the circus ring.

Because it was not always safe to be out on the table, he also kept food in the drawer. He had neat piles of celery, crackers, and cherries ready for whenever he needed them.

Yes, life in Sam's kitchen cupboard was comfortable enough—but it was always dangerous. Cato was sometimes afraid that if he were discovered, no one would recognize who he really was. John was forever snooping around, trying to look into the drawer. Cato sometimes had nightmares about being taken into John's house to be kept in a shoebox—like a mouse or a lizard.

There had been one night, one terrible night, when Cato thought John would surely catch him. He had been walking along the counter top and had just reached the side of the sink when he heard someone walk into the kitchen. Cato moved as fast as he could and reached the hole just in time.

A bright light flashed on above him. When he looked up he was dazzled. Then, behind the light, he made out two huge circles—John's glasses.

This very morning he had heard Sam planning a party. He knew that by evening the studio would be packed with people.

Cato decided that now, before the party guests arrived, he would slip out, have a bath and a big drink of water, and find some more food. Then he would come back to the drawer.

Tomorrow he would find a way of getting out of the kitchen before the building was pulled down. Then perhaps he could live in the wild like a jungle elephant.

He began to walk up the ramp. It would be good to splash around in some cool water and nibble at some party food before Sam's guests arrived.

Suddenly he felt a bump. His head had hit something. Puzzled, Cato looked up and discovered he had reached the top of the board. He had never hit his head before. He looked up again. Yes, there was the hole. All he had to do was keep walking—but something was stopping him. His head would not fit through the hole!

He tried to pull himself up with his trunk, but it was no use. He just could not get through.

He backed down the ramp and stood at the bottom. He was confused. He looked up at the hole and wondered what had happened. Suddenly he realized—he was growing! Hooray, he was growing! It must have started while he slept the night before. If this kept up he'd be his normal size again. Then he could go back to the circus—to hay and sawdust, and cheers and clapping.

But what if he only grew a little bit? What if he grew only so much that he could never get out of the drawer?

He paced back and forth, wondering what he should do.

Now he heard voices. Sam and John were coming into the studio with Mrs. Darcy. He could imagine exactly how they looked. Sam, long, lean, and bushy-bearded, John with his heavy eyeglasses, and Mrs. Darcy, cheerful and businesslike. Wouldn't they be surprised if they knew there was an elephant in the kitchen!

He heard more voices as Mr. Borrill and Stella arrived. Soon he heard laughter and music and glasses clinking. The party had started.

## The Uninvited Guest

Sam had never had so many people in his studio before. People sat on the bed, on the work bench, on the chairs, on the floor. Sam opened the big window, and people spilled out onto the lawn and even onto the sidewalk.

They talked, they told jokes, they laughed. They listened to music, they sang, and they danced (when they could find room).

When Sam looked around, he wondered if he had really invited so many. He asked John.

"Of course you invited them," John answered, opening a package of pretzels. "You went around town saying, 'I'm having a party tonight. Everyone is invited.' That's what you said. You invited nearly the whole town. That didn't surprise me. It's exactly what I expected you to do."

"So I did, so I did," Sam agreed as he swished

bottles around in a bucket of ice. "I know so many people—I didn't want to leave anyone out."

Mrs. Darcy moved through the crowd, telling everyone that Sam had given all his money to the Children's Home for a swimming pool.

She found Mr. Brown, from the council. "Do you know what my brother did? All the money he earned from his art show, the money he worked so hard for, he has given to the Children's Home."

She told Reginald Bisk, who was talking to Stella.

"That man will never be a millionaire," said Mr. Bisk, "but he will always have a million friends."

"I'm not at all surprised," Stella said. "That is just the kind of generous thing Sam *would* do."

Marjorie, from the newspaper, joined in. "That is the most heartwarming story we've had this year. I'm going to write about it in the paper. We might even put it on the front page."

Sam smiled happily as he looked around at

all his friends. *I'll never get that trailer now,* he thought. *I may never even have another studio, but who needs those when I have so many friends?*

Inside the drawer, Cato heard the sounds of the party. It seemed that everyone was having a wonderful time—except him. He tried to think of a way to get out of the cupboard drawer. The only possible way was to batter down the sides of the drawer. Although the cupboard was old and leaned to one side, it was made of very solid wood. Knocking the sides out would not be easy. It might even be impossible.

I'll try once more, he thought. I'll try to rip some wood off near the hole. Then the hole might be big enough for me to get through.

He stepped onto his ramp. He took a few steps up. The board began to bend. He went farther. Suddenly the board snapped in two. Cato crashed down onto the piles of colored paper. Coins, paper, cherries, brushes, and pencils scattered about the drawer, and Cato sat in the middle of them.

*  *  *

The party was as noisy and happy as a carnival. Everyone agreed that it was the best party the town had ever had.

"It looks as though half the town is here tonight," Mrs. Darcy said to Mr. Borrill.

"Yes, they must be—and the other half is across the street at my movie theater."

Sam soon decided it was time for supper. He brought out dishes of spaghetti, cold meat, and salads, and his friends set them on the work bench.

While Mrs. Darcy was helping with the food, Mr. Brown came up to her. "I have an idea," he said. "You seem to know a lot about committees and things like that."

"Yes, I do, I enjoy organizing things," Mrs. Darcy answered.

"You should become a member of the town council," Mr. Brown said.

Mrs. Darcy gasped. "The town council?"

"Yes," said Mr. Brown. "This council needs people who have a lot of energy and are not afraid of work. We need people who are interested in things that happen here."

"Well, I like the idea," she said.

"There's an election coming up soon. Try to get people to vote for you. Then you can help the town in all sorts of ways."

"I'd like that," said Mrs. Darcy.

Sam's guests began to crowd around the table for supper. John stood at one end of the table with a plate of food in his hand. He looked puzzled. He kept hearing bumps and bangs in the kitchen. Once, he had gone in there and looked—but he saw nothing unusual, so he came back to the party. He kept hearing things, though. Every now and then there would be a bump or a knock.

When everyone was eating, Mr. Brown walked to the end of the table and stood up on a chair. He gave a cough and knocked a spoon against a glass several times to get people's attention. Everyone turned and looked at him.

"Ladies and gentlemen," he began.

John heard Sam say to himself, "Oh, no, don't spoil the party with speeches."

"I don't want to bore you all with a speech," Mr. Brown said. "However, there is something which I feel you all should know. First, there is an election coming up soon in this town. Mrs. Annie Darcy has agreed to run for town council at the next election. As someone who has done so much for this town through her various committees, she will be very good on the council."

Everyone clapped.

"Next, my friends, I want to tell you about a most unselfish act. Our host, Sam Fleming the artist, recently held an art show, as you all know. The idea was to earn money so that he could buy himself a new home, perhaps a trailer, because this studio is being torn down."

Sam felt embarrassed. He didn't want everybody to know about his gift to the Children's Home. Slowly, as Mr. Brown spoke, Sam moved toward the kitchen door.

"Well," Mr. Brown went on, "that art show was an outstanding success. Sam made a lot of money, and he well deserved it. Now, my friends, listen to this. The Children's Home has no swimming pool. But they will soon have one. Sam has given all his art show money to the Children's Home for a pool. Let's all show our appreciation."

There was loud clapping and cheering. Everyone looked around for Sam—but he was standing in the kitchen doorway, with his back to the crowd.

As the cheering died down, there was another loud noise. It came from the kitchen. It was a splitting, crunching, cracking noise—sounds of breaking, falling, and smashing. The building shook. People stopped talking. They looked at each other with alarm.

The splitting and crunching sounds seemed to go on for a long time. Sam stood in the doorway staring into the kitchen. His guests just stared at his back.

Finally, there was another noise—a long, loud, trumpeting sound. It was the trumpeting of an elephant.

Sam turned around, his eyes wide with surprise.

"You'll never believe this, but there's an elephant in the kitchen."

Mr. Borrill ran to Sam's side, shouting, "Cato! It's Cato!"

They all rushed toward the doorway, trying to see into the kitchen.

"Sam!" cried Stella. "Your kitchen is in ruins!"

"Soon the whole building will be in ruins!" screamed Mrs. Darcy. "Everybody run!"

Cracks were opening up in the walls of the studio. The building was so flimsy that there was really no chance that anyone could be hurt. All Sam's guests ran out onto the lawn.

At the same time, the movie across the road finished, and the theater crowd poured out into the street. Seeing the excitement at Sam's place, they all rushed across the road to watch.

The empty studio was slowly falling apart. Then, with a final crash, the whole building fell to the ground, as though it were made of cardboard. All the time, the loud, happy trumpeting of Cato could be heard.

People were everywhere. They were on the lawn, all over the sidewalk, and on the road. The little studio lay on the ground looking like a heap of scattered matchsticks. In the middle of the wreckage stood Cato, nodding and swaying, with a merry look in his eyes—just as he had done at the circus. He was back to his normal size.

Mr. Borrill caught hold of Mrs. Darcy's hands and danced round and round. "I'm the happiest man in the world!" he cried. People were crowding around Cato, patting and stroking him.

Reginald Bisk, Marjorie, and Mr. Brown were standing close by, amazed at Cato's sudden appearance. The whole crowd buzzed with excitement.

John walked around Cato a couple of times, then stopped near Cato's back legs. Cato was standing in the middle of what was left of Sam's kitchen furniture. His right back leg was in a broken cupboard drawer. John bent down and looked closely. Cato was standing in a drawer full of money!

John hurried up to Sam, who was standing next to Stella at the edge of the crowd.

"Sam! Stella!" cried John. "Come and look at this!" They followed him to Cato's side.

"Just look at this," John said again, pointing

at the broken drawer. "You've been putting your wallet on that old counter top for years, Sam. Your money must have fallen into this drawer that was stuck. Look at it all!"

Sam bent down for a closer look. When he saw all the bills and coins, he jumped up and flung his arms around Stella.

"I'm rich again!" he cried. "I'm rich. I'm—well, not exactly rich, but—look at all my money. There's enough there to buy—to go to—oh, well, let's get married anyway."

# The Magician Who
# Changed Himself

"Cato, the circus elephant who disappeared three months ago, was discovered last night, not far from the old circus grounds, standing in the middle of what was left of a house belonging to Sam Fleming. So far, no one has been able to explain where the elephant has been all this time or what happened to Mr. Fleming's house. . . ."

Le Vram turned off the radio. He stared, unseeing, at the breakfast table. *I've done it,* he thought. *I've really done it. Not the Ancient Disappearing Trick. That's nothing compared to this. What I did was the Spectacular Reducing Event. That not a trick—it's real. I'm the happiest magician in the world!"*

He jumped up and danced around. "If I'm not mistaken, and if I remember rightly, it's on page 777 of *Secrets of the Ancients*."

He found the yellowed old book and lifted it down from the shelf. Flipping through it, he quickly found the page. There it was—all set out: the words, the gestures, the secret thoughts, and—at the end—this message:

"If ye would be evil, and cause sorrow, do this."

His hand trembled as he held the book, and he said, "I should be the happiest magician in the world. . . ."

Nobody ever *did* find out where Cato had been for those three months. John Darcy often thought about the strange rustlings and bumpings he had heard in the kitchen, the disappearing food, and the footprints. He read *Centuries of Sorcery and Magic* from cover to cover, but the ideas he got were so impossible that he would not believe them.

Reginald Bisk helped Mr. Borrill get the circus back, and Cato is the star again. Borrill's circus has become the biggest and most successful circus in the country.

Mr. Bisk decided that, since Cato had been found in Sam's kitchen, Sam was to get the reward money. With this, and the money found in the drawer, Sam had quite a tidy sum. He also found that a lot of the unopened letters in the drawer contained checks and money. These had been from people to whom he had sold paintings over the years. Some of the checks were still new enough to be cashed at the bank.

Sam and Stella got married. They bought a comfortable trailer and now travel with the circus. Stella enjoys being back in her old job. Sam is able to do a lot more circus pictures for Mr. Bisk to sell at his gallery in the city.

The Children's Home got the swimming pool, of course, and Mrs. Annie Darcy was elected to the town council. She has helped to make her town a happier and more interesting place in which to live.

Since then, the town has become famous. Marjorie's story of how Cato was found was published in newspapers and magazines all over the world.

* * *

In another town—not far away, up in the mountains—a certain Mr. Marvel has become very popular as an entertainer. He is especially in demand at children's parties, and often performs for the sick children in hospitals throughout the area.

Never again did he try the Spectacular Reducing Event. The formula in the book stated, "If ye would be evil...," and Le Vram no longer felt evil.

In his heart, Le Vram believed he really was a great magician because he had worked a rare, ancient magic. He had no need to be jealous anymore, so he changed his name, and decided that from then on he would try to make others feel as happy as he did.

Every day he makes children laugh and hears applause—just for him. People who had known him in the past would be astonished at the change.

Every year Borrill's Circus comes back to town for many weeks, because so many people want to see the famous elephant. Cato is in the ring, bowing and nodding to the audience at every show.

Mr. Borrill has discovered that many of Cato's tricks have improved, especially the one where he walks on a sloping ramp. As he performs, Cato's eyes twinkle—he is the only one who knows where he spent those missing weeks!